Preface

This book was written to inspire and empower generations of people to stop comparing themselves to others and to embrace who God created them to be. It is a reminder to never give up when life presents obstacles that seem impossible, to be aware of the importance of hanging around the right people, and to be humble, never seeking revenge, but instead Choosing to Rise Up and spread love and light to all.

I want to give a special thank you to Nossi College of Art & Design for making this dream of mine become reality, to Yancy Culp, founder of Spartan DEKA, for your support and all that you do to change lives around the world, and to Chris and Renee Fults, without you, none of this would have happened!

Thank you and God Bless!

Today's the day we've all been waiting for...

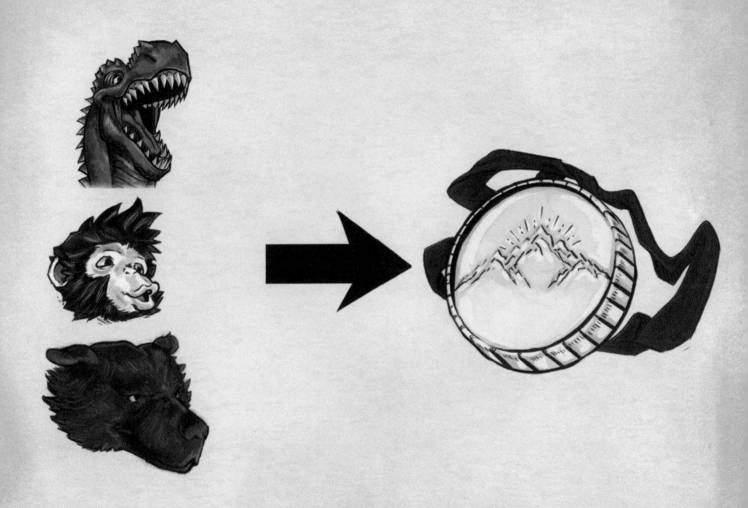

The best three athletes in the world. They have conquered the forest, trails, and international zoos. Today, they battle in a new territory for the ultimate gold medal!

Map

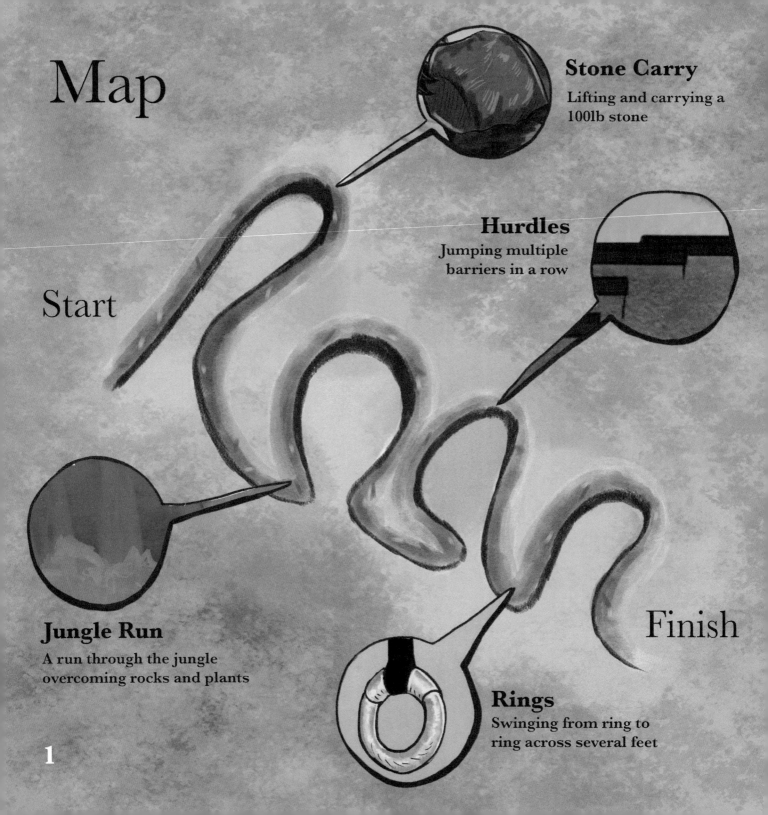

Stone Carry
Lifting and carrying a 100lb stone

Hurdles
Jumping multiple barriers in a row

Start

Finish

Jungle Run
A run through the jungle overcoming rocks and plants

Rings
Swinging from ring to ring across several feet

Tyler the T-Rex!

Fast, Dangerously Strong, and Powerful Jaws

Brandon the Bear!

Big, Strong, Fast, Powerful Claws, and Excellent Climber

Marco the Monkey!

Intelligent, Adaptable, Professional Climber, Confident, and Brave

2

Brandon the Bear and
Marco the Monkey
cheerfully walk to the start
line ready to race.

3

Tyler the T-Rex prowls into the starting corral with an ego full of arrogance.

4

Off They Go!

Coming out of the stone carry:
Tyler is in 1st, Brandon in 2nd,
and Marco barely behind.

7

Coming out of the jungle:
Tyler extends the lead and
Marco makes a pass into 2nd
place, but this race is a long way
from over.

8

A 400-meter run and over the hurdles they all go!
Tyler maintains the lead but Brandon makes a
move into 2nd place.

Into the rings, the final obstacle that's new to all of our competitors today!

Roar

Oh no...Tyler can't reach the rings... frustration is building!

11

Brandon approaches the rings but Marco, the professional climber, is only a few seconds behind.

12

Brandon makes it across and takes the
VICTORY! Marco crosses in 2nd place.
Tyler quits and pouts off the course.
Dino Dee tracks Tyler down.

Tyler the T-Rex agrees and
shows up to the retreat.

At Rise It Up Retreat, Tyler learns that he was
created to be unique and to be loved by God,
no matter whether he wins or loses a race.

Tyler learns that to become a
champion he does not need to
compare himself to others.
He is a T-Rex and just needs to
Embrace his Roarrr!

One Year Later...

The

Championship!
Attempt at Redemption!

It starts by remembering...
The most important thing you'll ever do
is the NEXT thing you do!

Tyler
the T-Rex

Brandon
the Bear

Marco
the Monkey

START

At the start line Tyler gets made fun of for
last year's failure due to his short arms.
Tyler stays calm and remembers his identity
of who he is and what he learned at
Rise It Up Retreat.

Off They Go!

21

Tyler the T-Rex takes off with the early lead.
Focused and locked in!

Coming out of the stone carry:
Tyler is in 1st,
Brandon in 2nd,
Marco in 3rd!

Coming out of the jungle:
Tyler extends the lead and
Marco edges into 2nd place
but this race is a long way
from over.

24

A 400-meter run and over the hurdles they go!

Tyler maintains the lead but Brandon makes a move into 2nd place!

25

Into the final obstacle where Tyler failed and was embarrassed last year...

THE RINGS

With a big lead Tyler approaches, leaps, and chomps through the rings!

27

Tyler the T-Rex takes the victory and earns the New World Record!

28

Brandon finishes in 2nd
and Marco in 3rd.

29

Brandon and Marco make eye contact with Tyler but drop their heads for being ashamed of bullying and laughing earlier.

Next time, join us at Rise It Up Retreat to *Embrace Your Roarrr!*

Meet the Illustrators

Hayden Hall

My goal is to become a successful artist and storyteller. I mainly contributed to the character design and the line art.

Instagram: hallistration37
Email:
stainway37@gmail.com

Claire Seiber

I have a focus on being very painterly in my art style and have a broad use of color. I contributed to coloring the characters and obstacles.

Instagram: cseib_art
Email:
claireeseiber@gmail.com

Gabby Lovelace

I'm a passionate and creative illustrator with a love for bringing ideas to life through visual storytelling. I contributed to the layout, art direction, and backgrounds.

Instagram: lovelacecreativeco
Email:
lovelacecreativ@gmail.com

About the Author

Considered as an expert at inspiring and empowering people and teams to embrace who they are in order to RISE UP and be the champions they were created to be. I was born in San Diego, California, have lived in Hawaii longer than anywhere else, and I call Tennessee home. I grew up in a single parent home with two younger brothers as a military kid moving around the country every three years. My upbringing brought many challenges, but I have learned to turn obstacles into opportunities and truly embrace who I am. That's been my key to RISING UP in all areas of my life. At the age of five, I was told by doctors that I would never be able to run long distance because I had lost 40% of my lung capacity. An Ironman triathlon, endurance race course records, and multiple ultra marathons later... I continue to defy the odds!

Based on my unique background as a Navy Officer, Spartan DEKA World Champion athlete, military funeral honors detail, Krav Maga and kickboxing instructor, and YoungLife/OCR for Christ ministry leader; combined with my impressive ability to see and bring out the best in people and situations, I use my unique story and life experiences to change lives and leave a legacy bigger than myself in this world. Sought out by universities, organizations, and sport teams to uplift and motivate their teams, I inspire people to "RISE UP" and conquer things they once thought impossible.

You can connect with me on Instagram (@bryanneely12), LinkedIn, Facebook, or at www.riseitup.org to learn more or to book me to speak to your group.

About Rise It Up

Rise It Up was created originally as a fitness and self defense training business in April 2021, but quickly became more of a platform to inspire and empower people to embrace who they are at the core and to live life to the fullest. Rise It Up is built on four pillars (faith, fellowship, fitness, and mindset) and they are intertwined into every product/service. Rise It Up's mission is to spread love and light to people all over the world, to create a community that inspires, supports, and empowers people to live more joyful and successful lives, and to provide retreats where people can go to be uplifted spiritually, mentally, physically, and emotionally.

Services Offered:

Coaching Services (Virtual / In person)

Inspirational and Motivational Speaking

Events (Retreats / Fitness Challenges / Community)

Rise It Up's Freeze Dried Treats (Healthy / Endurance Athlete Fuel / Candy Favorites)

The Rise It Up Creed

The Start to Winning Everyday!

My name is _____. I have a unique purpose. I am a Champion. I surround myself with other Champions. Today, I will give my all in everything I do. When I'm faced with an obstacle, I will keep my head up and find a way to win. I am in control of my mind. Today, I will Embrace My Roarrr because I am a Champion!

As a Champion,
I pick others up instead of putting them down.

Today I Choose to Rise Up!

Made in the USA
Las Vegas, NV
29 December 2023

83687126R00026